Alinda
of the
Loch

by
Oonagh Jane Pope
&
Julie Ann Brown

May all your dreams come true. JB

Published by

Across the Pond Publishing
Oonagh Jane Pope, Julie Ann Brown © 2009
www.acrossthepondpublishing.co.uk
www.acrossthepondpublishing.com

ISBN 978-0-615-28591-7

For information contact:
Oonagh Jane Pope
ojpope@gmail.com
Julie Ann Brown
profjulie@gmail.com

or visit our website

www.alindaoftheloch.com

Graphics provided by www.archivalart.com
Design (cover and website): Emelie Nystrom

Printed in the USA

www.V3corporation.com

Dedicated to our families

Rick, Andrew, Kirsten, Ruaraidh, Ewan

Paul, Jennifer, Christina

Acknowledgements

Alexander Patrick McElhaney
Bram Winter
Brittany Hazel Brooks
Christian Nicolai Thiesen
Christine L. Espinoza
Cody Raymond Sell
Dean Alfonso Buell
Dudley K. Laporte
Emelie Anna Maria Nystrom
Henrik Niklas Jonatan Falkenby
James Heaton
James Michael Constancio-lopez
Jessica Dorrine Marquez
Jonas Paul Martin
Kerry Lisa Smith
Kyran Alexander Million
Masahiro Noguchi
Megan E. Ackerman
Michael G. Mahoney
Ola Sterling
Ronald Vavro
Rosalba Guillen
Sam Julius Frankel
Sara Elizabeth Aaronson
Stephanie E. Flowers
Suzanna Noele Clark
Therese Elisabeth Lennefalk
Thomas Harrison Eisenberg
Tricia Lynn Grant
Whitney K. Lynd
Xiaoshan Liu
Zachary Adrian Shipman

Table of Contents

Introduction

B y the shores of Loch Ness in the Highlands of
Scotland, a majestic ruined castle stands, gracing a rocky
outcrop. The ruin, known as Urquhart Castle, clamours to tell her
tales. The past of this place with its legends of mystery and
conflict has been concealed, as the stones have tumbled and the
centuries have passed. For hundreds of years it has been the
home of warring clans and unseen kingdoms, but, as we shall
discover, the ruin is at last about to find peace with itself. On a
sunny day, the clarity of the views from the castle in all
directions is breathtaking, as striking mountains proudly frame
the site. A path leads from the north to an arched gateway, which
welcomes visitors in to explore the mysterious battlements.
Looking to the west a solitary tower stands tall, guarding the
furtive waters of Loch Ness.

All is not as it seems.

Lurking under the deep dark waters, full of peat and plankton, a shadowy creature patrols back and forth. It constantly keeps the ruin within its inner vision. Through the centuries, this creature has been heralded as both a monster and a myth. From far and wide the curious flock to the shores of Loch Ness, in anticipation of catching a glimpse of this elusive inhabitant of the loch. They are mindful of the danger the creature may pose if challenged. Imagine being the one to explain what lies beneath the water! Various descriptions and photographs have appeared in newspapers over many years – stories from normally sober citizens who are convinced they have seen the inhabitant of the deep. It has been seen to have one hump, two humps, even three humps. It has also been described as having a long slender neck ending in a small head. But until this tale unfolds no one will know for certain what lies beneath the water.

Long ago some schoolchildren told tales of a most peculiar and horrifying animal they had seen in a swamp in Urquhart Bay. They fled to their homes and refused to leave, unless accompanied by a strong and well-armed protector. Over the years these tales have been handed down and embroidered, and thus the legend has grown of the monster that patrols the loch and frightens those who get too close.

But too close to what? This is a clandestine mystery. What lies behind the tales, and why should such a creature be living in the waters by Urquhart Castle? The secret is hidden in deep dark caves right beneath the ruins. The secret is so precious that the monster will stop at nothing to protect it.

It is now time for our story to unfold.

Chapter 1

The Christening

Our story starts ten years after Queen Aurora and King Colin, rulers of Inverness-shire, had given birth to their twin daughters, Olivia and Shona.

This part of the land of the Scots had always been different, because their unusual acquaintances, the fairies, had enchanted it. The Kingdom in this story is where the tale of the beautiful, curious, and kind 'Sleeping Beauty' occurred. This particular piece of land, the water surrounding it and its people had been continuously touched by the unexplained and the often 'unseen' powers of the fairies.

In our modern world we find it difficult to understand how such tales could be more than myth. Through the passage of time the story of Sleeping Beauty has been transformed into a mere fable. However, this was a place where both good and evil have met and fought, both on the land (the reality) and in the minds of its people (the unseen).

Do you remember the fateful day of Aurora's christening from the tale of Sleeping Beauty? The day the good Fairy Godmothers and the evil Shadow Fairy met in battle over the future of an innocent baby. That child, Aurora, and her people suffered by having to sleep for 100 years, as a result of the wounded ego of the Shadow Fairy. Imagine feeling so keenly the rejection of being not being invited to such a very important event. This wound was so deep that it made her inflict harm on that blameless baby, without a shred of remorse.

After the Shadow Fairy's horrific conduct at Aurora's christening, where she laid her curse, the Fairy High Court met to decide on the future of the fairy who had brought disgrace to their kind. They deliberated on what should be the fate of the evil creature. After much heart searching, her fellow fairies banished her to a bubble of lost liberty, where she was to be left floating through space and time. In this bubble her magical powers were rendered useless. She was sentenced to witness and experience the happiness of those she had tried to destroy, through the magic of an aperture to reality. She would not be released from her prison until she showed full remorse for her crimes. Her freedom would only be secured when the light of empathy and compassion had cleansed her dark self.

The whole Kingdom slept for those long 100 years. When finally released from the evil spell, many years of happiness occurred for Aurora, as she married her charming rescuer, Prince Colin, and gave birth to twin girls, Olivia and Shona. Aurora felt at peace knowing that Shadow was walled in space in a transparent prison. She put all thought of the evildoer into the dark recesses of her mind and concentrated on living life to the fullest with her beautiful family.

However, everyone underestimated the anger and resentment of the Shadow Fairy. During those long 100 years in captivity, Shadow gained in strength and resourcefulness. She plotted and planned to escape her prison, determined to exact revenge on the family whose very being had locked her away for so long.

Now, at the end of a celebration party for the tenth birthday of the twin princesses, Aurora announced some wonderful news. She told her husband that they were to have an astonishing gift, a new baby. Colin was overjoyed and together they planned their future to include this surprising addition to their family.

Months passed and at last the baby was born. She was another girl to complete their family. The baby was beautiful with piercing blue eyes and hair the colour of apricots, which shone like a halo crowning her head. It was apparent from the beginning that she was a special child whose sunny disposition caused her parents few sleepless nights.

A few weeks after the baby's birth, Aurora called her family together to make a special announcement. 'It is time to arrange the christening of our precious daughter, whom we will name Alinda. We must organise our guest list.'

She kept deep in her soul her thankfulness that the Shadow Fairy was securely imprisoned. She could not have borne a repeat of the torment of the 100 years of deep sleep that she and her Kingdom had suffered through the jealousy of one wicked fairy.

Aurora would not have felt such peace of mind if she had known of the plotting indulged in by the Shadow Fairy. Alone for so long, she had kept sane by imagining how she would free herself and exact revenge on the happy family. Knowing that only true remorse would bring about her liberty, she transformed her thoughts through sheer will into light and loving feelings, but underneath her heart still dwelt a deep dark soul.

Meanwhile, across the Kingdom and after much deliberation in the Fairy High Court, it was decided that the Shadow Fairy was to be released to the Land of Lessons Learned in the furthest region of the Fairy Kingdom. There, she would be under the guidance and instruction of those known as the Virtue Fairies. On the fateful day of her release from the bubble, she was immediately taken to the Land of Lessons Learned, accompanied by two sentinels. During the transportation process Shadow used a special spell she had spent years perfecting. The spell created a perfect duplicate of herself, while the real Shadow became invisible to her guards – so she was free to roam, while her duplicate took her instructions in the Land of Lessons Learned. Its flaw was that should she be discovered she would revert to one being … her original self!

Her duplicate was a model student who fooled her teachers into thinking she was excelling in her transformation. In the meantime, the real Shadow Fairy was gaining strength and readjusting to life outside of her prison. All the while she was planning on how she would destroy the happiness of those living in Urquhart Castle. The christening of the new baby would be the perfect opportunity to darken the lives of the royal family once again. Aurora, she believed, would never recover from the pain that she would inflict upon her. Shadow held that thought joyously in her black heart.

On the day of the christening the bells of the castle chapel were ringing tunefully to herald the beginning of the prayers and celebration for Alinda. On hearing their sound, three Virtue Fairy Godmothers arrived, bearing their gifts for the baby.

They were unconcerned that their student, Shadow, would cause any havoc at the event, as they had left her practising her virtues under heavy guard. They were very much mistaken.

The light streaming through the stained glass windows filled the chapel with a rainbow of beautiful colours, reflecting the love and joy that filled the hearts of all who were present. After Alinda was baptised the three Fairy Godmothers stepped forward to give their gifts.

Faith Fairy gave the gift of fortitude.

Hope Fairy gave the gift of optimism.

Joy Fairy gave the gift of bliss.

All seemed well in the glen. Then suddenly silence fell all around, the light dimmed, darkness engulfed the chapel and a sense of dread filled Aurora's heart. Instead of the bells ringing to mark the ending of the christening, an explosion shook the building and a shower of multi-coloured stained glass flew in from the largest window in the church. It announced the arrival of Shadow. Knowing that she did not have much time to place her wicked spell on Alinda, she flew towards the royal party, grabbed the infant from her mother's arms and screeched,

'My gift to you is that upon your 18th birthday, you will go into a deep sleep for 500 years. If another from your Kingdom endeavours to join you in your slumber, or tries to reverse this spell, you will instantly die.'

Aurora, horrified by this wish, grabbed her baby back from the Shadow Fairy and held her tight, trying too late to shield Alinda from the evil presence. In that instant, the energy needed to sustain two beings, in the guise of herself and her duplicate, and the manifestation of such an evil act, caused the Shadow Fairy to combust and turn into dust. All her years in captivity had not taught her that good always triumphs over evil!

The hushed and horrified guests watched, as, with tears in their eyes, the Virtue Fairies dramatically blew the dust out of the chapel into all the corners of the Kingdom. The Shadow Fairy had cast her last immoral enchantment.

Unlike the fragility of her spell at Aurora's christening, this time the Shadow Fairy had planned the details meticulously. Years passed, and though many tried, every effort failed to reverse or eliminate the dreadful gift. Consequently, the King and Queen decided that they would make every day special with their family, and they prepared for life without Alinda.

Chapter 2

Growing Up

Alinda grew up to be a sensitive and creative person. Her sisters married men of strength and wisdom. When they had children, Alinda delighted in spending time with her niece and nephew. As they began to talk they affectionately called her Auntie Bliss. This was because of her consistently happy and devoted nature. Indeed the whole Kingdom loved her.

Since she had been a wee lass, Alinda had spent much of her spare time designing unusual adornments for her dolls. Once, when she was eight, she angered her mother by using some of the royal jewels to create a crown for her favourite doll. The gems shimmered and shone and gave her doll such style that Alinda was justifiably proud of her creation. Her enthusiasm was somewhat dampened by the ire of her parents who were aghast at the temerity of their daughter in playing with such valuable treasures. However, even though they were upset, they realised that Alinda had an obvious talent. Therefore they decided to foster her young mind and creative imagination. They provided her with a tutor who nurtured her passion by providing her with both tools and knowledge to further her artistic gifts. They were full of pride for the creative instinct of their beautiful daughter, and treasured her talents.

Shona also recognised the originality of her younger sister's thinking and asked her to make a dress for her wee baby girl.

'I would love you to make something special for Jane's birthday party. Would you sketch out some designs?' she asked.

'I will try,' enthused Alinda, 'I'll go and make some sketches straight away.' She danced with the lightest of footsteps

11

on her way to her room in the south turret. The sunbeams poured into her room through the small rectangular windows and bathed her rough wooden table in glorious illumination.

The Princess spent hours creating a plethora of designs. She eventually decided on an extravagant red gown that she would embroider with semi-precious stones. She had to spend a great amount of time trying out new techniques in order for her plans to work. Her parents were amazed at her dedication and tenacity. The tower, looking out over the deep dark loch, was a perfect place to spend time creating the dress. As she sewed, she often glanced out at the hills on the other side of the loch and dreamed of a future filled with dazzling patterns and colours. The family watched her with wonder and often went to sit with her, just enjoying her presence.

However, their pride was tinged with sadness and desperation over Alinda's future. Colin and Aurora went far and wide seeking all manner of solutions by seeking any wise wizard, witch, fairy or troll who might have had the knowledge to help them reverse the evil spell placed on their daughter. But there was no remedy. Each night before they went to bed, her parents would pray that Alinda would be spared from the dreadful fate that awaited her and themselves. They did not know how they would be able to bear the pain of a future without their child. A future that would have Alinda sleeping in suspended animation, still close but unattainable, while they tried to carry on with a normal life. Their time with Alinda was precious and seemed so fleeting.

However, the reality of their situation was not lost to them, and so, during the years closer to her birthday, they began to plan for Alinda's slumber. Aurora spent the last year before her beautiful daughter's awful fate, gathering together articles which might comfort her. She could not bear to think of her daughter lying in some dark place for 500 years … locked in a living death with nothing familiar surrounding her. Therefore she thought carefully, and planned relentlessly, as to which objects to place near her to bring comfort to her daughter when she awoke.

An artist was commissioned to paint cameos of herself, Colin, Shona and Olivia. These were attached to a necklace that was to be a gift for Alinda on her 18th birthday. Aurora wondered with anguish whether Alinda would be granted the time to receive the gift before succumbing to the wrath of the Shadow Fairy.

Chapter 3

18th Birthday

Alinda had been anticipating her 18th birthday with pleasure for some time because she had a surprise for her family. She had met a handsome man, the previous year, who she believed was to be her one true love. She had met him in the south when she had accompanied her friend Lady Isla to a clan celebration. They were visiting Isla's distant relations who had invited a young friend, Prince Andrew, from a nearby castle. He was very enamoured with the young Alinda and they had found they had much in common. Since their first meeting Prince Andrew had joined Lady Isla and Alinda on several picnics, and they had fallen in love. Alinda had invited both Andrew and his family to her birthday party in order to introduce him to her parents. How surprised they would be about her news! (Of course, she had no inkling about the fate that awaited her.)

Her special birthday dawned with a typical bright Scottish morning. Dew sparkled on the grass around the castle, and the air was crisp and fresh. The sunshine peeping through the tower window shone on her face and awakened Alinda. Such a beautiful day filled her heart with joy and added to the excitement at the prospect of sharing her celebration with her family, friends and, of course, Prince Andrew!

The first visitors of Alinda's day were Aurora and Colin. They told her to dress and come downstairs into the garden as they had an unusual present to surprise her with. Alinda was very curious as she contemplated what it could be. She quickly dressed and rushed down to meet them. There, to her surprise, were her mother and father playing with a baby dragon! She had never seen such a creature before. On seeing her, the little dragon ran to greet her, and jumped up into her arms. Colin and Aurora stood back and watched with some sense of comfort in knowing that the small animal was to be her protector through the centuries that were to follow. Although they had accepted they could not change her fate, they wanted her to be as safe as they could possibly make her, and the dragon would play her part.

Alinda had always loved to sit by the water near the castle and play in its peaty edges and thought perhaps the creature would like to do so too. Debating as to what she should call her new friend, she decided to name her Nessie after the loch that she loved. Calling to her whole family, who had congregated to see what the commotion was about, she ran to the shore to place Nessie in the water in front of the castle. The creature splashed around with exuberant enthusiasm and when she became tired, as babies do, Alinda picked her up in her arms and took her back to the garden where she could sleep.

Her birthday was full of fun, food and laughter. There was no hint of the sorrowful event that was predicted to befall the family and the Kingdom that day.

Had Shadow's gift failed? Glimours of hope entered Aurora's heart when nothing happened to spoil the morning. Perhaps the death of Shadow had also killed her spell?

The guests began to be announced at midday. The King and Queen of Lachlan, and their son Prince Andrew, arrived with more than just gifts for the celebration. Having already discussed his wish to make Alinda his bride with his own parents, Andrew approached Colin and Aurora to ask permission for her hand in marriage. Alinda's parents were stunned! They had never anticipated such a dilemma. They were delighted at the prospect of the match of two such prominent Scottish families. However, they said they would need to take time to discuss their answer. How could they explain to Andrew's bewildered parents the reason for their hesitation – that of their fear for Alinda's immediate future? How could they put into words their dread that she was still under Shadow's spell?

In the presence of Prince Andrew, Alinda's heart pounded. He was dressed in the kilt bearing the tartan of his ancestors and was as handsome to her as she was beautiful to him. She looked forward to their lives woven together like the pattern of thread in his tartan. She was not worried that her parents had not given their immediate consent to his proposal, as her parents were not given to swift decisions regarding matters of such importance to the kingdom.

As the night grew late and the guests began to beg their goodnights, Alinda felt a sense of fatigue. She believed it was because her day had been so full. However, before she retired to bed, her parents and sisters had one additional surprise for her. It was the cameo necklace her mother had commissioned, which had, painted on each part, a picture of each of her family members. Her mother put it around her neck and lovingly kissed each of her cheeks. Alinda said she would wear the precious gift always. It was so beautiful and would remind her of just how much her family meant to her. She hoped that in the future there would be another cameo added to the necklace with a picture painted of her beloved.

Alinda said, 'Goodnight,' and thanked her parents for a lovely birthday. However, she sensed that they seemed somewhat unusually sad that such a perfect day was about to close. She told them that she had had the most perfect birthday celebration and that she too wished the day would never end. The Princess climbed into her comfortable feather bed and shut her eyes. Those beautiful blue eyes would not open again for 500 years.

Chapter 4

A Scottish Holiday

'Are we nearly there?'

Grant and his sister were bored to tears and were desperate to arrive at their destination. They had begun their day early as they had arrived at the airport in plenty of time for their flight. Then there was the short trip up to Inverness airport where they and their parents waited impatiently to pick up the hire car they had ordered. Finally, they travelled through the glens to their holiday retreat, which was a beautiful private castle on the shores of Loch Ness, which their parents Robert and Rebecca had hired each summer for the past three years.

Jumping out of the car, the children dashed down past the castle to the loch's edge and hunted for stones to throw in. The sun glinted on the loch and the green hues of the trees reflected boldly in the clear water. It was a beautiful day. Grant noticed a new addition on the waterside.

'Look!' he cried. 'A pier.'

His parents laughed. 'It's a jetty, Grant.'

'I had an e-mail the other day explaining that we will now have the use of a boat to explore Loch Ness and perhaps use to fish. The owners of the castle feel it will enhance the experience of this place,' explained Robert.

The family loved the peace and privacy of the Scottish Highlands. It was a world away from the life they lived in England. Robert was a rock star, continually hitting the top of the charts with his band, and he lived life at a hectic pace.

Much of the rock music his band played was created in the sound studio at his country estate, but they played gigs all over the world. Therefore each year his wife insisted that they retreat to a peaceful place away from their frenetic existence. His work meant that many people vied continually for his time and energy, and she often thought there was little emotion left for his family. This precious holiday in their small Scottish oasis was just what they needed to bind them as a family again.

There was a boat sitting tied up to the jetty – a lightweight motor cruiser.

'We will go out in the boat tomorrow, kids, as long the loch is calm. We must take care out on the water,' said Robert.

'You're not scared of the monster are you?' asked Kirsty with trepidation in her voice. She was not sure she wanted to go out on water that had the reputation for harbouring monsters. Each year she had been at the castle, she had spent some considerable time on the roof of the North Turret gazing out on the water hoping to view the creature. She had even asked for a camera for her birthday that year as she hoped to catch a glimpse of Nessie and take a picture of the elusive creature. It was not easy being the daughter of a famous rock star and she thought this scheme might be a way for her to receive some attention from her Dad. Kirsty spent a lot of time dreaming of becoming famous also.

'Of course not, Kirsty,' said her Dad. 'There is no such thing as a monster. We will be quite safe.'

Kirsty felt downcast and frustrated at her Dad's comments. She was sure the monster existed and she hoped her camera would help her prove it!

For the next few days, the family explored the area around the castle, enjoying the fine weather and spending many hours in the Scottish sunshine. It was such paradise to be on the estate where there were no prying paparazzi to document their every move.

The daily routine began each morning by taking a short trip in the boat, practising manoeuvring it till they were sure they could navigate their way safely back to the castle. Finally, much to the delight of the children their Dad announced, 'Tomorrow we will take a longer trip. I will ask the housekeeper to make a picnic up for us and we will go over to Urquhart Castle.'

Rebecca, their mother, was keen to see the castle ruin as she had done some research on it. She discovered that there was a landing jetty alongside the castle where they could moor their boat. Both children were filled with excitement at the prospect of the trip and went to bed voluntarily!

Early next morning the family set off on the outing, with high spirits and the anticipation of a great adventure. They cast off and made their way up the loch in a westerly direction. On both sides of the loch, heather clad hills rose tall and majestically. Areas on the hills revealed exposed boulders and high cliffs. Seeing them, the children imagined and played out battles of the past – fierce Highlanders dressed in tartans with weapons of rough hewn steel popped into their heads, and they talked of how the brave warriors must have battled to the death. Thus they happily spent the journey steeped in the past.

Suddenly, as they cleared a headland, the majestic sight of Urquhart Castle loomed up ahead. The children, already curious about Scottish history, wanted to know all about its glorious past. Rebecca spent the remainder of the journey telling them stories about the colourful inhabitants who had lived there.

As Robert moored the boat the children tumbled on to the jetty ready to explore. Their parents told them to stay where they could see them and choose a spot for their picnic. After the journey they were ready to eat and have a rest. The housekeeper had packed a magnificent picnic, which they ate with pleasure. Then after lunch, with Robert and Rebecca sitting enjoying the sunshine, the children went off to explore on their own.

'Don't go far,' they were warned, 'and try to stay together.'

Chapter 5

The Discovery

Kirsty wanted to take her camera to the highest vantage point of the castle to look for Nessie. Grant showed no interest in joining her as he was far more interested in exploring the nooks and crannies of the old castle walls. So they parted company and agreed to meet back at that spot in half an hour.

He went off down the eastern side of the castle, exploring the undergrowth there. Imagine the thrill he experienced when he discovered a shallow entrance to a dark space behind castle stones that were covered in moss and protected by overgrowing vegetation. It looked like it had not been disturbed for years so he decided to take a closer look. As he squeezed into the space, he found himself in a dark tunnel, and as he moved forward a bright light reflected in his eyes from further into its depth. Taking a deep breath, he decided he would follow it to its origin although he knew this was not the safest thing he could do. However, Grant was a daring boy who did not get a great deal of freedom at home so he carried on. The tunnel became narrower; taking him deep under what he guessed was the centre of the castle.

As he finally approached the light, he saw it was emitting from a source that was surrounded by several large stones. His heart pounding hard in his chest, he decided to press himself behind the stones to see more of the light. It was a difficult task for a small boy but he was on a quest and would not be defeated. Exhausted but triumphant, he was finally able to see that the light was actually a reflection of a tiny ray of the sun which somehow found its way into this deep spot. He could see that it was landing on what he thought was dirty and imperfect glass which stood at the front of a cave. He thought it strange to find this there, so he reached out and rubbed the glass with his hands. He was amazed to see that it had something inscribed on it, even more so to find he was able to decipher some writing.

It said

PRINCESS ALINDA OF INVERNESS-SHIRE
AGE 18
BORN AUGUST 31st 1509

Grant recoiled a little, fearing he had discovered the resting place of a Highlander who had died at the hands of the warriors he and his family had talked about on their way in the boat. He did not know how he would feel should he discover a skeleton. But being a boy of intrepid bravery, curiosity got the better of him and he decided to disturb this princess's resting place. He cautiously moved further into the cave. Despite small pieces of rock falling all around him he realised he would have to remove additional stones to see what was hidden. Imagine his shock when the last stone he removed revealed the perfect face of the Princess. She appeared to him as if she was sleeping, but he realised she was encased in a glass coffin and was wearing clothes which he knew from museum visits came from a bygone age, so that would be impossible. He gazed down at her, taking in the smooth waxen white skin of her beautiful face, her perfect mouth, her hands lying limply by her side, and marvelled that her body remained so real.

Life as a rock star's child had taught Grant the value of discretion so he backed away, replaced the stones, crept back through the passage and emerged through the undergrowth to the outside world. He decided to maintain her secrecy. He knew if he mentioned this discovery to anyone, she would become a spectacle for the press from all over the world to hound and embroider stories about. As she had obviously been there for a very long time, he decided that this quiet dark cave was the best place for her to remain.

Meanwhile, Nessie, the Princess's guardian dragon was intuitively shaken. She had grown into a huge monster and remained elusive over the centuries, but she was alert to danger for her mistress. Sensing that Alinda had been discovered, the creature rushed through the waters to swim into the submerged hole, which led to the entry to the underground cave. It was here she had lived, protecting the Princess from harm for almost 500 years!

Kirsty, meanwhile, had been scanning the loch from her castle vantage point. Suddenly a massive dark shadow under the water swam with devastating speed into her view. She pointed her camera with shaking hands and took several photographs of the beast under the loch. To her eyes, the shadow of the creature seemed to merge with the land almost underneath her, and then disappear. Kirsty waited for it to swim out into the loch again but she was perplexed when the water remained still and the silhouette did not reappear. She called out to her brother, who was emerging from the undergrowth way beneath her. She ran down to join him as fast as she could, and began telling him about her adventure, all the while paying no heed to the fact that his face told that he too had a story.

As they returned to their own castle in the boat, Kirsty kept on retelling her Nessie story and examining her digital camera display. Unfortunately only she could see the shape of the monster on it, as the waters of the loch are deep and dark, and they merged with the monster to create a dark splodge on the photographs. Robert and Rebecca comforted her saying, 'There is bound to be another opportunity for you to get that photograph, you will be luckier next time.'

In the meantime, Grant was in a dreamy state, thinking about Princess Alinda and planning when he could next visit too. He thought to himself that he could come each year near her birthday to coincide with the family's annual visit to Scotland. Did he really find a lost princess today?

During the following years he did indeed keep his promise, and visit Alinda. He revealed to her his innermost thoughts about his family, friends and his life in England. He imagined that she listened to him and he grew fonder of her with each passing year. He considered her to be his greatest secret and a confidant who would never divulge what he told her. It is rare and refreshing in the modern world to have such confidence in a fellow human being, especially when living within the maniacal lifestyle he experienced from his father's fame in the music business.

Chapter 6

Centuries Lost

Many years later, after a gap of some summers, Grant was back in Scotland to attend a house party that his father was throwing to celebrate his 25 years in the music business. Rebecca suggested their old holiday castle for the location and decided on a renaissance theme to stun their friends with. Their guests were required to wear clothing for the weekend that reflected the chosen theme.

Kirsty, now grown up and more interested in social activities than monsters (she had long ago got over her disappointment of the black pictures instead of the monster she was so sure she had seen), took great delight in planning outfits for herself and her friends. Millicent, who had been her friend for years, in particular wanted to look stunning. She had been trying to impress her friend's brother Grant since she had started to notice boys. This evening, she anticipated, was her chance to make him sit up and realise she was no longer just his wee sister's friend, but someone whom he could take out and romance.

Grant realised the date of the renaissance ball was in fact Alinda's birthday. He was excited at the prospect of visiting her, although he felt guilty at the lapse of his promise, as he had not seen her for the last few years. The family had not made their annual visit to the Scottish castle once the children had grown up and started holidaying abroad. He decided he would take her flowers to celebrate her birthday by way of an apology. He could not imagine what the others would say if they knew that he had his very own renaissance princess.

On Saturday morning the castle was a frenzy of activity, so Grant was able to slip quietly away to the jetty, wanting to be on his own, and take the boat out to Urquhart Castle. On his way there, unbeknown to him, Nessie began to follow him, sensing danger for her Princess.

Grant left the boat, with the flowers in his hand and joy in his heart at the thought of seeing her again. He was relieved to discover that the entry to his secret place had not been disturbed. He made his way in, only this time it was more difficult since his grown up bulk was considerably larger than his boyhood size. However, he persisted and, on reaching the cave far under the castle, he began to remove the stones he had replaced there to screen her from discovery. Moving the stones was a lengthy process but he spent the time reminiscing about the first day he had made his find.

Finally he was staring at Alinda, lying inside her glass coffin and looking exactly as he remembered her. He drank in the features of her lovely face and marvelled at her beauty. He began to tell her all about his life since his last visit then began to sing to her, rather self-consciously, 'Happy birthday to you.'

As he was staring down at her, finishing his song, he imagined for moment that he saw her move. Thinking it was a hallucination born out of wishful thinking, he tried to steady himself as he put the flowers on the encasement. At the precise moment the flowers touched the glass, Alinda's eyes opened and he saw that fear engulfed them.

Grant thought quickly and immediately picked up a stone to break the glass coffin to set her free. Alinda began to scream in total confusion, as she had no idea what was happening. Grant, full of fear himself, said to her, 'Please don't scream Alinda, I won't hurt you. Please let me help you.'

Although shaking from both cold and fear she found the courage to ask him in a strong Scottish brogue, 'How do you know my name? What am I doing here and who are you?'

Grant was both shocked and hurt by the tone of her questions. He replied, 'I found you nine years ago, buried in this coffin under Urquhart Castle and have done my best since that time to protect you from the outside world. My name is Grant and I have no more idea than you what is going on.'

After hearing his answer she became even more confused. Why had she been here for nine years and why did he look and sound so strange? Suddenly she heard a desolate cry from the unbroken side of her glass case. It was a dragon's call. She immediately remembered the gift she had received on her 18th birthday yesterday, and knew that it was her dragon calling for her. She began to try to break the rest of the glass that surrounded her so that she could get over to Nessie. She was certain that the dragon was her protector and that she was crying in pain with her. Perhaps they could comfort each other and Alinda could make sense of what was happening.

Grant, seeing that Alinda was attempting to break more of the glass while calling to the creature, decided to help her. He, in fright at the appearance of the fierce-looking dragon, warned her that perhaps the dragon was to be feared. 'That creature is the Loch Ness Monster and people have been trying to find her for years,' he told her. 'I think we should stay clear of her.'

She said to him, 'Nonsense. She is mine and will not harm me.' So Grant helped Alinda break through the remaining glass. They could see a large cavern that not only contained the dragon and access to the loch by an underground stream, but also many objects that Alinda recognised from her past.

They moved carefully into the cave where Nessie came to her and rubbed her head on her owner's outstretched hand. Alinda, although amazed at how large she had grown, told the creature that she had done well in protecting her. Her size told her more than anything that something momentous had happened to her and in fear she looked around. She told Nessie to go into the water and wait for a while as she must spend time looking around her cavern to see if there were clues to help her discover why she was in this situation. When she had worked out some answers she would come and call her once again. She vowed to comfort her devoted dragon for she was full of thanks for her obvious faithful service.

Chapter 7

The Letter

As she looked around her, Alinda realised that natural light from the cave was enough to silhouette many of the objects she saw, but she needed more light to see them fully. As if reading her mind, Grant told her he had a new type of device that would light up when turned in a specific direction. He held out the flashlight he had brought with him to light his way, and showed her how it turned on and off. Rather than being shocked by the apparatus, she said, 'Thank you. I am grateful such a tool exists so that I can see what is around me.'

With flashlight in hand Alinda began shining it around the room. She noticed that there were several large metal trunks. Grant came to help her open one of the trunks, but when he touched it, he received a sharp shock from the trunk and was suddenly thrown backwards. He was unhurt and Alinda immediately worked out what had happened.

'It is most likely enchanted,' she said. 'I am certain that I will be the only one who can open it.'

Before she tried to touch the trunk, she closed her eyes and clutched one of the cameos that hung on her necklace. She opened her eyes then let go of the cameo. She touched the latch and the trunk opened immediately. The Faith Fairy had served her well.

Within the first trunk she found a letter from her Mother and Father and her prayer book and beads. She also saw several sacks of gold and silver. Finally, she found her Mother's jewellery box and, as she opened it, was flooded with memories of playing with it during her childhood. She found a letter sitting on top of the jewels, so she carefully closed the lid of the trunk, sat down slowly and began to read. The letter said:

Dearest Daughter,

Today, you have awakened in a strange place and time. I know you are weak and confused and above all frightened that you are without us. If there were a way we could cross time and space to be with you, I promise you, darling daughter, that we would be there at this very moment. You will realise we are unable to do so, and therefore we need to help you, if possible, to understand what has happened to you

You will remember that I told you that when I was your age I had awakened to find myself 100 years in the future. I was confused and weak and wondered where I was and who was with me. With your Father's sweet kiss I was awakened with the rest of my Kingdom from the slumber they had shared through the century with me. This will not be the case with your awakening, Alinda.

Just like it was with me, a slumber spell was placed upon you on your Christening Day by the same wicked fairy who enchanted me. It was a spell to put you to sleep for 500 years and would occur on your 18th birthday. She wanted to be sure we would never be together again. The Shadow Fairy died shortly after your christening. Had she lived we would have done our best to have her remove her curse from you.

We did try during your entire young life to find a spell to reverse the incantation. All manner of sages and fairies were asked to find a cure. We were told that the evil energy of the spell, prepared with numerous calculations, made reversal impossible. Shadow also had made the spell impervious to any attempt to make changes. We were then left with a choice – to tell you or let you remain happily with us in ignorance. We tried to weave many happy moments for you during your life to sustain you in whatever challenges are facing you now.

I can tell you that Faith Fairy said she would never give up trying to find a way to get you back. Her plan is to bring you back to us through time. Once the spell has run its course, Faith has created the only spell possible to get you back. She has arranged that at the end of your second year of awakening, on your birthday, you must come back to this cave at midday. When you arrive here you are to take a mirror she has enchanted and wait for her to appear to you inside the mirror. You will find the mirror in the narrow gap of rock behind the third trunk. If Faith Fairy has succeeded in her plans to have you return home, she will be able to take you back to us.

We have left you with many treasures from the days of your life with us. The greatest is your necklace as it will constantly remind you of us. Our love crosses time and space and never changes. We have also left you with three trunks. The first contains gold and silver for you to survive in the world, and some pieces of my jewellery which you so dearly loved to play with. This jewellery may help you in ways we cannot yet imagine. In addition I had a special cameo of Prince Andrew created for you to place on your necklace. When you disappeared he searched frantically to find you. We could not tell him of the spell or of your location for fear that he might try and disturb you. It has been difficult for both him, and us, but was necessary if you are ever to come home again. The second trunk contains fine fabrics and gold, which we hope will help you to support yourself. The third trunk contains mementos made for you by your sisters who are missing you dearly.

Nessie, as we are sure you will sense, is your special guardian. She will remain by your side over the centuries to protect you, and will create diversions from all manner of dangers that may befall you. When the two years are over and you make a choice to come home or stay, the creature will be free to live her life no longer in service to another. Until that time, when you are near or in the castle you will be safe from discovery.

Finally, darling daughter, your Father and I will continue to visit you throughout our remaining years. When we see your sweet face we will offer up prayers for whatever path you choose when you awake in the distant future. We appreciate that you may decide to stay in the world that now seems unfamiliar to you. We just ask that you tell Faith Fairy of your decision. It is your happiness that we seek. Dear Alinda, stay strong through continued use of your special gifts of optimism, fortitude and bliss.
With all our love,
Mother and Father

Chapter 8

The Masquerade Ball

After reading the letter out loud, Alinda cried solidly. Grant knew that consolation would be impossible, although he would dearly have loved to comfort her, and so he waited until she was ready to talk.

'You can't stay here. Come with me and I will make sure that you will be safe,' Grant offered, when her sobs finally quietened.

The Princess, now exhausted and still confused, felt she had no option but to trust this kind stranger. Grant picked up several pieces of her jewellery and asked her to select a dress. Knowing she would need something to wear for the ball that night, and working out that she would not look out of place, he helped her choose an outfit suitable for the evening. Alinda called to her friend and protector, Nessie. She lovingly stroked the dragon's face and told her not to worry as, with Grant's help, she would come back the following day.

Grant showed Alinda the way out of her secret place, which had kept her so secure for all those years. On reaching the outside she breathed in the fresh air, and raised her face up toward the sun. She felt totally joyous at the freedom of movement and drank in the views of the Scottish Highlands. At first, it seemed that not much had changed, until she was shocked to focus on the ruined walls, which marked where her family home had been. Calling on her Gift of Fortitude, she deliberately pushed all thoughts of the past to the back of her mind, then followed Grant down to the jetty and got into the boat.

Throughout the journey back to Grant's holiday home, Alinda began to ask many questions about life in his century. He in turn questioned her about her experiences growing up so long ago. Their free flowing conversation made the journey pass quickly and before they knew it, they were tying the boat up to the jetty.

Grant's thoughts were racing as to how he could create a cover story for Alinda. Realising his parents and sister would be curious about where they had become acquainted, he decided to ask Alinda to say they had met at Urquhart Castle museum where she worked as a guide.

As they entered the castle the ball was in full swing. Grant realised that he needed to change but looking at Alinda knew she was dressed perfectly. Imagine her appearance. She was wearing a gown she had designed and sewn 500 years before. The gold threads shone as brightly as when she had stitched them, sitting at the crude wooden table in her turret. Its bodice was laced tightly and the long skirt hung beautifully from her waist. On her feet were simple sandals made from leather and her hair, pinned up on top of her head, was full of little ringlets.

Grant took Alinda up by the back stairs to a guest room on the second floor, where he asked her to wait while he changed for the ball. He placed her jewellery pouch on the dressing table and left her.

She walked around the room looking at and touching in amazement all the wonderful and strange objects surrounding her. Then she opened her mother's jewellery box and gently took out the special headpiece, which she placed with reverence upon her head. She had created and embroidered it to wear during the afternoon festivities that were held on her 18th birthday. She had considered it to be her best creation yet, a masterpiece, and its very sight brought back memories imprinted in her mind from what seemed to her like yesterday. How had she not sensed that her life would forever be changed on that day?

The headpiece had designs of flowers that were embroidered with gold, copper and silver threads. As unique as it was, the matching jewellery she now placed round her arms and on her ears was even more unusual. She remembered she had worked with a court glassmaker and silversmith for months to make her exact design. She had created in gold and glass the matching necklace, bracelet and earrings that would reveal her innovative style. However, as she had vowed back then never to remove the cameo necklace given to her by her beloved parents, she carefully left the second necklace sitting on the desk in the room.

Hanging on the wall in front of the desk was a large ornate mirror. She went over to the mirror to make sure she had placed her headpiece correctly. As she looked at her reflection, she was flooded once again with memories. She closed her eyes and felt the joy she experienced when she had worn the jewels for the first time.

On opening them and gazing into the mirror she did not see what she undoubtedly was – a beautiful apricot blond, with piercing blue eyes and skin of the palest porcelain – but she saw instead a lost princess hiding her unhappiness under a dazzling crown.

She felt herself being held together by a string of familiar tokens from the life she lived long ago. She tried to convince herself to be grateful that she had been found by Grant and had not woken alone. Everything, she believed, could have been much worse. She decided she really needed those christening day gifts given to her by her Fairy Godmothers.

She would behave at tonight's ball with the conduct she knew her parents would expect of her, the invited guest of her new friend, Grant, calling upon her Gifts of Fortitude, Optimism and Bliss.

With that thought in her head she heard Grant knock on her door. On entering, he asked if she were ready to be escorted down to the ball. He was totally stunned by the beauty of this Princess. However, he was careful not to betray his thoughts and perhaps overwhelm her by his attentions, so he just held out his hand. Taking a deep breath Alinda strode through the open door, gave him her hand, and together they descended the spiral staircase ready to face the world.

As they reached the top of the main staircase Grant looked down and felt as if he, too, had awakened in a different time and place. The grand hall was professionally decorated to reflect an event held by a royal family of the past. His parents had spared no expense to make the occasion appear authentic. He thought to himself that it really must be similar to what Alinda had experienced when she lived at Urquhart Castle, albeit without all the trimmings.

He gently released her hand (which he had held in a way similar to those he had seen in period piece movies), then stopped and looked at Alinda. In the past years when he had gazed on her face it was like looking at a portrait. Now, she was a living and breathing woman and he did not want to let go of her hand or stop looking at her face. He had to mentally shake himself to return to reality.

Alinda looked around the room beneath her. She thought that many of the objects within her sight looked unreal. Everything seemed so strange. The people appeared similar to those of her past but were more polished and perfect. The fabrics and patterns worn by most of the women were completely foreign to her, but they excited her greatly. The styles, she noticed were both familiar to her yet different. She decided that the adornments especially had no place in her memory. She felt keen to learn about those around her, so she began asking Grant questions.

As he was answering yet another enquiry, Kirsty and her best friend Millicent suddenly appeared. Kirsty (like all sisters who want to know their brother's business) was curious as to

38

where had he found Alinda, and how he had convinced her to be his guest. Her brother was usually not so lucky with women.

Alinda blushed at the comment and Grant went into his story about how she was working as a guide at the castle. Kirsty, before moving on to other guests, finished with a quick comment that she would love to know more about Alinda's clothes. She particularly liked the headpiece and earrings and said it would be good to steal them.

Meanwhile, Millicent, who was speechless with rage and despair, said nothing as she watched Grant look adoringly at the strange girl in the beautiful clothes.

Grant noticed that Alinda was quiet after his sister had jokingly used the word 'steal'. Just as he had thought, Alinda was confused at the way they had commented on her attire, and the general manner in which women and men spoke to each other. He told her that his sister was being what in his world was 'funny', or a joke. She thought to herself that adjusting to this strange modern life was going to be much more difficult than she had imagined.

After meeting Alinda, Millicent was filled with anxiety, confusion, and anger. She could not believe that after all these years Grant had met someone special. She had hoped tonight he would notice *her* in the gown she had carefully planned for weeks to wear to attract him. She had thought he would see her with different eyes in her beautiful dress. Instead, she felt once again invisible to him, just his little sister's friend. Through her dismay, she thought to herself that there was something strange about his date. Perhaps Alinda was after the money she thought he must have through his family. She had realised that one of the reasons he had not had a serious girlfriend in the past was because he feared he would only be loved for his father's money and status, and not for himself. She decided she would not give up. She had loved Grant since they were children. They had known each other for as long as she could remember as both their dads were in the rock band. Millicent was convinced he should trust her much more than someone he had just met.

When in anger and misery and consumed with jealousy, the human heart may react out of character. Thus was the case with Millicent.

She surreptitiously watched Grant and Alinda throughout the long evening, rocked to her soul with envy of the beautiful creature who had so suddenly appeared in their lives. She realised that Alinda was most unusual and the snatched conversations she heard between them gave her the feeling there was something about her that did not add up. Millicent had recently left university with a degree in journalism and she convinced herself that here was a story worth pursuing.

Throughout the evening, Alinda found herself becoming more and more disorientated. As the music grew louder it pulsated through her whole being, the guests seemed to become more frenzied and shrill, her senses became overwhelmed and her head filled with pain.

Her daily childhood 500 years ago had been simple and mostly quiet. The most exciting events then were connected to the weather or the animals they kept, with the occasional ceilidh at local landlords' homes interjected into what, to most in the modern world, would have been a mundane way of life. This evening, which had begun with such promise, now took on a totally different dimension.

She felt threatened and vulnerable but was unsure why she felt like that. Grant was protective and kind and his friends and family had shown her politeness and quiet interest, so there should have been nothing for her to fear. As she thought back to her happy childhood years she realised that no shadow of evil had ever before entered her senses.

However, now that she knew what a victim she had been at the hands of the Shadow Fairy, she questioned whether she could have developed intuition of evil intent, through a change to her psyche. Deep in thought she became suddenly aware of a ghastly voice whispering in her ear.

'I don't know where you have come from but you don't fool me. Grant has been mine since I first saw him and there is no way you can come in here and take him from me. I will find your secret and destroy you.'

Chapter 9

Flight

illicent had no way of knowing how disquieting her words were and how deeply they would affect her rival. The noise, the frenzy of colour, the movement from the dancing, and now this veiled threat from an unseen source, filled Alinda with such a blind panic that something inside her snapped. She lifted her skirts and took flight, battling her way through the hoards of people until she was finally breathing in the pure Scottish air she recognised from her childhood. She found herself standing by the loch and the boat she had arrived in was moored right in front of her. All her instincts drove her to run to the familiar. So she jumped in the boat and, as she had seen Grant do earlier, started it up and sped up the loch.

The night was clear and bright and the full moon graced the loch with a soft eerie light. As she headed homewards she saw, to her relief, a large dark figure swim in an arc towards her – her beloved protector was ready to guide her to safety. Nessie glided effortlessly to turn just under the water in front of her, and together they made their way back to Urquhart Castle. Alinda moored the boat and ran back to her cavern, all the while sobbing quietly in despair and relief.

Meanwhile, back at the party, Grant was frantically searching for Alinda. He had been aware of her taking flight through the ballroom and had realised that the whole evening was probably too much for her. Kicking himself for his greed in wanting to have her company for the evening, he castigated himself as he found his way to the pier. He was devastated to find the boat and Alinda gone, and, understanding that she would have returned to her roots for safety, he jumped in his car and drove round the loch to find her.

Millicent had watched the drama unfold and was excited at the thought of finding out more about her rival. She got into her car and followed at a discreet distance behind her adored Grant. She had no idea of what she was going to do once they arrived at their destination. She was reckless about the fact that she might be discovered and encounter his wrath at her spying. Thoughts spinning through her head were born out of love not reason. Her whole emotions had been spent planning how she and Grant would come together as a romantic pair that evening, and she was mortified at the way the things had turned out.

As she realised they were in fact heading for Urquhart Castle, where he had said Alinda was a guide, her thoughts turned to how she could observe where he went without revealing herself. Grant turned into the castle car park and getting out a pair of cutters, snipped the padlock on the gate, opened it up and drove through. Millicent on the other hand, dimmed her lights and parked her vehicle before running down the long track to the entrance of the castle. In front of her she saw Grant bear off to the right, rather than head straight in to the ruin, and she followed him down its side. To her immense surprise, she saw him walk through what appeared like a wall of stone covered in vegetation, and disappear. Creeping in to the space he had vacated, she found herself in a long dark passage. Summoning up all the courage she possessed (as walking into the unknown is a test of hidden attributes), Millicent was rewarded with the sound of voices way up ahead. When close enough to hear what was being said, she stopped, then eavesdropped on Alinda and Grant's private words. It took much pinching herself to convince her that their conversation was a serious one of sleeping princesses and fairy tale lives. She listened until she felt she had gleaned enough information, then feeling excitement growing in her soul and afraid she would be discovered, retreated back to her car to await the next events.

Alinda and Grant spent some time talking over the evening and although she told him most of her feelings of chaos, she did not mention the threat by someone who was a friend of his or his parents, wanting to spare his feelings. Nessie surprised them by crying and calling to them but they did not heed her too closely, thinking her just pleased to have Alinda back. She told Grant she would like to spend some time alone in the cavern, thinking over the events of the tumultuous day, and they agreed he should collect her the following day.

Alinda assured him that she would be quite safe with Nessie there by her side and he left her reluctantly. However, he too needed time to think about the momentous events of the last hours and the drive back to Inverness would give him time to organise his thoughts and have a reasonable explanation for his parents to explain his disappearance from the party. Driving guiltily out of the gate he had broken through, Grant did not notice the car sitting in the top car park and drove carefully home. He found it hard to believe the events of the day but he was full of hope that he would play a large part in Alinda's future.

The ever-awake society of this century played well into Millicent's hands. As she drove home she alerted a friend in the press to the story of a strange girl who had appeared from a forgotten time, and who was living in a cave beneath Urquhart Castle on the shores of Loch Ness. No more information was needed, as the whiff of a famous story in the making was worth the gamble that this was perhaps an elaborate hoax. A tale about a monster might have been more credible (although that had been played out before), but a girl who had come through time? No matter how improbable, such was the recent flow of bad news that perhaps a fairy tale was just what the nation needed. The media descended on the castle in hoards and by lunchtime the following day the area was awash with newsmen. There was even a helicopter hovering overhead, reporting on the chaos brought to the normally calm and tranquil glen.

Grant was horrified to see all the activity as he drove into view of the castle the next day. Although he had heard on the radio that there was a problem, he was unprepared for such a crowd. The whole charade brought back to him his childhood fear when the press would not leave his father alone. He was turned away by a local policeman who told him firmly that he could not park anywhere near Urquhart Castle, such was the danger to the general public of the vehicles that had brought the news hounds. Highland roads are narrow and winding and were not built to cope with such activity. In despair he drove back to Inverness with the idea of finding a boat to take him there. Of course the boat in which he had so idealistically taken Alinda to the ball was moored by Urquhart Castle.

Inside the cavern, Nessie became very agitated and woke up an exhausted Alinda to warn her of peril. Looking into the mirror left to her by the fairies, she saw what was happening outside and knew she was in real danger of discovery. Her first thought was she had to protect her cavern as without it how could she go back to her own time, if indeed she decided that was what she would do. She needed the two years given to her by the wish to make an informed choice. She therefore knew she had to flee and rushed to Nessie, indicating to her that she wanted to leave by the loch exit. Totally trusting her protector, and with her fairy gifts to arm her, she jumped on her back and clung tightly to Nessie's neck. The great monster plunged into the tunnel, which led her to the loch, and together, protector and princess, they made their way out to safety.

Meanwhile, the disappointed media could find no evidence of a princess, and one by one they left the area to pursue more lucrative stories. Millicent was mystified why they had not been able to find the entrance to the cave, but knew there was nothing to be gained by revealing herself as the source of the supposed Lost Princess. The power of a parallel universe had beaten her this time!

Grant, on the phone with a directory at his side as he searched wildly for a boat to rush to Alinda's aid, was hugely relieved when a dripping wet princess sneaked in to the house through the back entrance. He could not believe how pleased he felt to see her safe. He realised how important she was becoming to him.

Chapter 10

Crossroads

S everal days after the grand ball and her momentous escape, Alinda was most surprised to receive a phone call from one of the guests she had met briefly. She was a famous rock star known as Pisces, and she had admired the headdress and jewellery that Alinda had worn to the party. They had chatted at the event and Pisces had been impressed that Alinda had designed the distinctive pieces herself. She was going on a tour to Europe with her band and wanted Alinda to create her something special to go with the outfits she was to wear on stage. Of course Alinda was delighted that Pisces thought her designs were so exquisite and immediately agreed to meet her to discuss some ideas.

Grant was amused as he watched the two heads bent in concentration over a large sketching pad and listened with pleasure to their conversation. The contrast of the golden hair of Alinda, and the jet black hair of Pisces made a sight to behold, and he was entranced watching and listening to them. He realised this girl who had come into his life was getting into his unconscious mind, and he worried that he was falling in love with her. In the uncertain world she was living in, would Alinda choose to stay here when her time was up or would the draw of her family be too strong for her to fight?

He put all thoughts of the future to the back of his mind and decided to live for the moment.

'What are you two up to?' he enquired. 'I didn't know you were friends.'

'This is a business arrangement,' Pisces told him. She was very taken with the gentle and polite manner of Alinda, recognising in her a unique flair. She thought her to be a little unusual and wanted to help her develop a business, which would support her and further her creative talents. Pisces knew she was an icon to many people, and the clothes and accessories she wore on a tour were always copied and duplicated in high street shops. She was excited to have discovered Alinda's accessories because she knew she also would gain extra publicity from such unusual adornments. Pisces was an acute businesswoman, as well as a talented singer, and was aware that stardom could be short lived. She was keen to maximise her potential by reinventing herself as often as she could, to keep her fans interested in her and her music, and this gentle soul would help her in her quest.

Over the next few weeks the girls became firm friends as well as client and entrepreneur. Alinda immersed herself in a world of creativity, just as she had done in her past life, and was astounded by the advances that had been made in the production of jewellery and adornments. Grant introduced her to modern materials and tools that enabled her to create unique designs, which resonated with her royal heritage. This heady mixture of past and present was exactly what Pisces and the modern marketplace were looking for.

Alinda spent the Christmas season with Grant and his family at their country estate in England in a whirl of social events. She was often the centre of lively conversations as people were drawn to her magnetic personality. Also, once the beautiful handmade headpieces and jewellery she wore were seen, they were never forgotten. They shone and sparkled with a wonderful aura, enhancing the holiday spirit. However, the constant attention Alinda received did not fill the void in her heart. She missed her family dreadfully. At times her memories overwhelmed her and she found herself seeking solace in quiet spaces.

Grant felt as if he had been struck by a double-edged sword. Although Alinda was constantly by his side, he felt she was as unattainable to him as when she had lain cold and silent in her class cage. He had been hoping throughout the last few months that his feelings for her would have been returned, but instead he knew she still considered him more like a best friend. He feared her heart remained in the past with her beloved Andrew, and her family. However, he decided she was worth fighting for.

After the new year, Alinda found herself in a frenzy of activity. She spent every waking hour designing and creating ever more elaborate fashion for Pisces' European tour, which was due to start on Valentines Day. Above her London apartment, which Grant helped her to find, was a loft that she rented for her business. She hired local art students as temporary staff and together they learned – Alinda about life in the present, and the students about art from the past.

Grant decided to take time out from his career to accompany the girls. He did not want to waste one part of the two years that Alinda had been given in this modern world, as he was certain he could win her love. The more he knew Alinda the more he was growing to want her to be with him always, and he was convinced that he would be able to keep her in his time. As soon as she realised his attributes, Grant knew she would know he was the perfect match for her!

It seemed that, almost before Alinda's feet had touched the ground, Pisces' European tour was ready to begin. Her debut performance in Paris was a sell out. The combination of a new album release and her new look on stage catapulted both girls into the spotlight. Their faces appeared on all the popular media worldwide so anonymity was lost to them and global fame was their reward.

The most alert media hound recording their every breath was Millicent. She was still intent on exposing Alinda's great secret and watched her with quiet menace, while pretending to be her friend. Her love for Grant consumed her and although they met regularly, he still just regarded her as his little sister's best friend and treated her as he did his sister. But she was convinced that patience would reward her when Alinda slipped up and revealed her hidden secrets. However, as time passed, her goal of revealing Alinda and landing a scoop became less important than losing Grant. The months on tour accompanying Alinda had ironically brought herself and Grant more together.

Chapter 11

Contemplation

Alinda slowly grew tired of the life of a modern day princess. The constant travelling and interviews, the parties, the press attentions (although at first attractive and novel), grew wearisome. When Pisces excitedly announced the tour was going global, Alinda knew she could not sustain the pace it would require. She craved the peace and solitude she had experienced in her turret of Urquhart Castle.

Alinda said, 'Pisces, I am very happy that you have been offered this opportunity, but after the European tour finishes in Glasgow this summer, I won't be coming with you.'

Pisces, although not fully surprised, responded with sadness in her voice, 'Why?'

'I just feel I am losing my creative edge as there is no time or space for me to create and test new designs. I am so grateful for the opportunity you have given me, and to have you as my friend. I hope I will not disappoint you with my decision,' replied Alinda.

Pisces had realised that the gentle nature of her new friend did not lend itself to the world of rock and roll, therefore she understood Alinda's announcement. The girls hugged and agreed they would still keep in touch and work together on future projects.

That same day, during lunch with Grant, Alinda told him that she would be leaving the tour when the European part finished in July.

'I have been wondering how much longer you would stay with this kind of life. What do you think you will do?' Grant asked anxiously.

'I'm going to go back to London. I think I would like to work on a few special pieces through commission work. I have had offers from several celebrities to make special pieces for wearing at the Oscars next year. And several clothing designers would like to enhance their catwalk collections with my work. I have grown weary of my celebrity status and just want some peace and solitude. I have loved travelling and experiencing this modern magic, but it's time for a break.'

'I think I understand how you feel,' said Grant. 'I have been watching you closely recently and thought you needed a break, Alinda. So I talked with the agents last month, and have rented our usual castle by Loch Ness for the whole summer. I was hoping you would come with me after the climax of Pisces' tour. It's not far from Glasgow, and as I know how much you miss your home, you will enjoy a holiday in the Highlands. Then perhaps you will be ready to return to London.'

Beyond that time the pair did dare voice their innermost feelings.

Alinda was thankful for Grant's thoughtfulness. He often seemed to be able to read her mind. She wondered what would have become of her had she awoken alone that fateful day. Just as she was pondering this question, Millicent walked into the restaurant and saw them. Her heart sank seeing them looking so happy together, but she put on her false persona and approached them with what appeared a friendly spirit. They invited her to join them as Alinda had grown fond of Millicent and enjoyed her company. (How easy it is to show a false face!) Alinda shared her plans with Millicent about leaving the tour and said she would miss their friendship.

Sensing an opportunity to keep close to her, Millicent said, 'Alinda, I would like to offer my services to you as your press secretary. I could also assist in developing and marketing a website for your work.'

Alinda did not need much time to think over the offer of the chance to work with Millicent because of the sense of reassurance she felt with her. Although she thought Millicent did not know her whole history (how wrong she was), Alinda had known her since the first day she awakened into her current life, and she knew Grant trusted her. Therefore she took no time to decide that they would make a great team.

Chapter 12

Back to Loch Ness

Alinda created an amazing jewelled tartan headdress for Pisces for the final concert in Glasgow. Everyone who attended the event immediately shared their fascination with this new style, wanting to buy into the new trend, and reinforcing her need for Millicent's expertise. As a result, before leaving with Grant for their holiday, Alinda asked Millie, now renamed, as a softer kinder girl had recently emerged, if she could join them in order to develop their business strategy. Grant was dismayed as he thought he would have his princess to himself, as he was planning on that summer being the make or break time for Alinda to fall in love with him.

The morning after the hugely successful concert Alinda and Grant set off for the Highlands to stay at their holiday retreat by the shores of Loch Ness. They had already decided to take in the beauty of the glens by travelling up the western route. It took them through Glen Coe. Alinda had travelled the same journey 500 years before and was surprised how little had changed. The landscape was exactly as she remembered it, with wild and dramatic hills bordering each side. Memories filled her mind of the picnics she had enjoyed with Lady Isla and Prince Andrew. Behind her sunglasses she hid her tears from Grant and was immersed in her own thoughts for many more miles.

Suddenly she was aware that the car had stopped, and looking down she realised that before her lay the castle of her birth. In the twilight it looked surreal, lit up by strong spotlights, and as she gazed at it, she easily imagined herself back in time. She asked Grant if they could walk down to the ruin but was disappointed to find it was too late in the evening and the castle was closed. He put his arm around her to comfort her and said, 'Don't worry, we will have plenty of time in the next month to visit your home. We can come as often as you would like in the boat.'

As they drove along the last few miles of the loch side, Alinda could clearly see that Nessie had sensed her presence and was shadowing them up the loch to their destination. This made her heart leap as she anticipated their reunion.

During breakfast the next day on the patio, Alinda and Grant both relaxed and enjoyed the view of Loch Ness while the warmth of the sun kissed their skins. Alinda, for perhaps the first time, stopped and really looked at Grant. She had not noticed that he was rather attractive and had an engaging smile. As if he sensed her thoughts he smiled and said, 'We are going to have an amazing month.'

The housekeeper asked what time would they like to have their lunch. Grant requested a picnic, as they would be out for the day. He then turned to Alinda and told them of his plans to take the 'Official Tour of Urquhart Castle'. He hoped they would be able to slip away for their picnic and then visit her cave unseen, as there were always many visitors to the popular castle during summer seasons.

The tour provided Alinda with great amusement, as she felt there could be no guide on the planet that knew her old home better than she. It was hard to keep her knowledge quiet! After the tour ended Alinda suggested the perfect spot to eat down by the water. As she lay down the blanket, they looked to the loch and could see Nessie moving towards them. Nessie lingered but did not surface, sensing discovery if she came too close to the shore.

After their lunch, the couple carefully walked round the side of the castle checking all the while to make certain no one could see them. They slipped quietly into the secret opening and went down the passage into the cavern. Alinda was ecstatic to be back and immediately went to the water and called out for

Nessie. Grant enjoyed watching the reunion of monster and maiden. When Alinda was ready she turned to him and said she would need help in deciding which objects to take with her to aid her with her new career in London.

Grant said, 'I think you need to take only a few things today that we can carry out without arousing suspicion. We will come back and collect anything you want over the holiday.'

Together they happily explored the chests, the first of which was filled with several small bags of gold and silver coins. The sale of these coins would finance Alinda comfortably for the following year and give her the opportunity to pick and choose the cream of her commissions. Her thoughts turned to her parents and again she was thankful for their insight in their preparations for her new life. She picked the finest stones to take with her plus one bag of gold. Then Alinda bade farewell to Nessie and the cave and they carefully left by the secret entry.

Wakening very early the following morning, Alinda slipped out on her own (leaving a note for Grant), took the boat from its moorings, then set on up the loch with Nessie alongside her. She arrived at the castle well before its official opening time. Alinda looked forward to spending the whole day in the cavern with Nessie, her books and her other belongings. This would be the first day she had been by herself in many months and she spent it between laughter and tears. On finding the dress she had worn on her birthday, a vivid memory of herself and Andrew caused her to weep so much that she lay down and sleep overtook her.

When she woke up, she decided she wanted to find out any information she could about Andrew and how he had lived out his life once she had left him. She felt great distress in knowing how much pain he would have suffered on her disappearance, after announcing they were to be married on her fateful 18th birthday. Later when she returned to the holiday castle and Grant that evening, she found him in a rather anxious mood.

'Alinda, I have been worried about you all day. I would really have liked to have been with you,' stated Grant.

'I needed time alone with my memories,' she replied. 'I have a favour to ask you. Would you be willing to drive me to Castle Lachlan?'

'Is that the castle where Andrew lived?' he asked.

'It is.'

'We can go tomorrow,' said Grant, although he was full of trepidation over her request.

As Alinda said an early goodnight, needing to sleep after her long emotional day, Grant decided to do some research on his ghostly rival. What he found would change the course of their relationship.

Grant awoke early and knocked on Alinda's door.

'If you get dressed and come down quickly, we will have plenty time to visit Castle Lachlan today. It is a lovely day and I have arranged for a picnic which we can have there.'

On the journey down through the glens, Grant asked Alinda for other suggestions of what she would like to do that summer. All she wanted to think about was Andrew, but she made the effort to consider other places she had visited during her youth that she could share with Grant. Privately he wondered if he was doing the right thing in encouraging all these thoughts of the past into her head, but he hoped it would help her to make the obvious decision to stay with him when she had to make her choice.

Alinda's excitement grew as she recognised the hills and glens she had once walked through to reach Andrew's castle. She closed her eyes and pictured herself with Lady Isla (her best and trusted friend) and Andrew eating their rustic picnic on a day much like this. It was full of sunshine, fresh air and hope.

When she opened her eyes she gasped. Instead of seeing the ancestral castle, she was horrified to see ruins in a much worse state than her own old home. The remains sat on a peninsula that could only be reached when the tide was out, but, as Grant had done careful research, he had planned their visit around the tides.

They made their way to the ruins. Alinda pointed to a very old tree in the distance and said, 'Under that tree was the best moment of my life. It was there that Andrew asked me to be his bride.'

Filled with jealously and anger, Grant threw caution to the winds and decided to tell Alinda from his research of the night before that he knew exactly what had happened to her former fiancé after she had fallen prey to the wicked Shadow Fairy's spell.

'Last night after you went to bed I did a little research on Andrew's life. He married a woman named Isla and they had four boys. It appears they were loved and respected by their clansmen,' he told her.

She tried not to show her shock at this news, but her sense of betrayal was so immense that Alinda lashed out at Grant and her ring caught the side of his face leaving a permanent reminder of that moment for both of them. Seeing his blood brought her back to her senses, and she begged his forgiveness as she tried to wipe away the blood with her scarf.

He said, 'Neither of us has shown themselves in a good light today, so let's call a truce and go home.'

Over the next few days they slowly repaired their wounded egos and they forgot their row. They began to share more intimate moments. Grant, trying to make amends for his hurtful comments, suggested she visit the cavern more often to fuel her creative juices, and enjoy time with her pet dragon.

Meanwhile, he threw himself into planning a surprise birthday party for Alinda. He contacted his sister and Millie and asked them for help. He also invited Pisces, his parents and some of Alinda's students and her friends to the event.

Alinda felt differently the next time she went back to her cave. She was no longer the girl who yearned for her old love. She was now the woman who had to make an important decision about her future knowing that Andrew had found a new love. She had always assumed she would return home after the two years had passed but now she doubted that thought. Perhaps Andrew and Isla had always been meant for each other, and maybe she was destined to stay literally a world away from them both.

Thoughts turned round and round in her mind. She was very uncertain about interrupting the past. What damage might she do if she went back to her own time? Had Andrew desperately tried to find her when she disappeared? Had he always been attracted to Isla? Would he still want her if she took the fateful decision to walk back through the mirror?

From its hiding place she removed the enchanted mirror and willed it to give her guidance on what to do. It remained silent and as she stared at her own reflection she realised that only she had the answers to her future. Once again she would have to access the Gifts of Fortitude, Optimism and Bliss, given to her at her christening by the Virtue Fairies.

Carefully placing the mirror back in its hiding place, she took out the letter and touched the necklace from her mother that had always remained with her since her discovery. She sat down in the cave reading time and again the portion of the letter that said:

'We realise that you may decide to stay in the world that now seems unfamiliar to you. We just ask that you tell Faith Fairy of your decision. It is your happiness that we seek.'

She read it one last time and made the decision that she no longer believed Andrew was her one true love and that he would be waiting for her to return. She grasped his cameo from the necklace around her neck and tore it off. She threw it into an open trunk.

This symbolic gesture gave her a sense of power and energy that would fuel her strength and continued success in what might be her final year in the modern world.

Chapter 13

One Year Gone

As Alinda lay in bed feeling the warmth of the summer sun hitting her face from the open window, she made a birthday wish. She wished that on this day (which was starting out in a similar fashion to that of 500 years ago) she was 18 again with her whole life before her.

Of course this was not to be the case.

She stepped back into reality as Grant knocked at her door and called, 'Time to wake up, birthday girl! You have a great day ahead of you.'

Alinda decided in that moment she would choose to be happy on her birthday and in the year to come, as her fate was in her own hands. She would live in the moment.

She let Grant know that she would be down shortly and that she was looking forward to hearing him sing her that 'Happy Birthday tune.' She felt a surge of contentment fill her as she gave thanks for her happy circumstances and the people who had welcomed her without questions and made her feel she was family.

As Alinda came to the kitchen table she was greeted with hugs and kisses from Kirsty and Millie and Grant's mother.

Grant also came up and hugged her. He was surprised when she hugged him tighter and longer than she had ever done before. He even more shocked (but definitely happy) when she kissed him on the cheek and whispered, 'Thank you for making my birthday begin with such happiness. I really appreciate having you in my life.'

He was so stunned to hear her words that he was not the first to start to sing 'Happy Birthday' to Alinda. He eventually joined in the song with feelings lighter and happier than he had experienced for some time.

After a long breakfast Alinda said that she wanted to go for a walk in the country. Grant quickly said he would like to join her. Everyone around the table noticed that Alinda had a smile and a warmth around her that they had not seen before.

Millie was certain she knew what it was that was making her so happy on her birthday. Alinda was beginning to respond to Grant in ways that were not based on pure friendship and brotherly love. It was what Millie had hoped would never happen and out of fear she responded to Alinda, 'I think after that large breakfast I could use a walk, too.' Turning to Kirsty she asked, 'Would you like to go with us?'

Kirsty laughed and said, 'You bet. I will go and change my shoes and meet everyone outside.'

Grant was disappointed that he would not be alone with Alinda during the walk. He thought that it might be the only time during the day that they would have had a chance to be alone. He found himself irritated by Millie and her quickly chiming in with a desire to join them for a walk. He was sure that he had mentioned to her (as he considered her such a good friend) that he wished he could spend more time alone with Alinda. So he decided that he would have to talk with Millie soon so she would respect his wishes.

To get over his annoyance, he focused on the firm hug and sweet gestures he had received that morning from the woman that he wished would love him. The impact of her actions lingered in his memory throughout the day and he realised he was the one who was having, ultimately, a very happy day.

After the walk the girls prepared for a day of shopping and adventure seeking. Alinda decided that since this was going to be the start of her new attitude, she might as well splurge and purchase some new clothes and shoes. She had been so busy working she had spent little of her wealth on herself. This was going to be another change in her life.

She decided that she would become in a way, 'her very own prince charming'. She smiled as that thought crossed her mind. 'This modern world offers freedom in ways that I never believed could exist.'

It was not such a bad place or time, just different. It was going to be a good birthday. She was happy from the inside out.

The girls enjoyed their day of shopping in Inverness. They had a great lunch and began planning their next activity, which was the Urquhart Castle tour. (Grant had planned well to keep Alinda away from the preparations for her party). As they drove into the car park Kirsty said, 'Every time I come to the castle I remember seeing Nessie. I wish that picture I took had come out. No one ever believes that I did see the monster. I would really like to prove it!'

Alinda secretly hugged herself with the knowledge that she had the power to make Kirsty's dream come true! As they began the tour, Millie remembered that Grant had said Alinda was once a guide at the castle. Throughout their conversation that morning, that fact had not been mentioned.

'Alinda,' Millie asked, 'tell us about the castle.'

Alinda told them the original history of the castle. She did not realise that she was being deceived, as Millie was storing up the details to enhance her story, should she ever need to tell it. Alinda finished by telling them of the love story of her mother and father.

Kirsty and Millie were surprised to find that this was the fabled 'Sleeping Beauty's castle'. They teased her by saying that she must have made up many tales like that one when she took the visitors on castle tours.

'Oh, no!' said Alinda. 'The story is true. Queen Aurora and her King were known far and wide as being the symbol of what true love means for Scottish people. If only you had seen how much they loved each other, you would instantly believe in the power of love.'

'It sounds like you were there!' said Millie mischievously.

They had at last reached the top of the familiar turret that Kirsty had climbed when she was small. Before Millie could ask any more questions and much to Alinda's relief, they were interrupted by Kirsty suddenly screaming in glee, 'There it is! I can't believe it ... It's the Loch Ness monster coming in our direction. Where's my camera?'

Alinda closed her eyes and sent careful messages to the monster. She asked her to come just a little closer and stay above the surface for a few moments then submerge and immediately hide in the cavern.

'I got the picture, I got the picture,' yelled Kirsty.

On hearing Kirsty yelling, people rushed to see what all the commotion was about.

'I have a picture of the Loch Ness monster ... Look ...!' she shouted.

Alinda was relieved that she was no longer the centre of attention. Castle staff and tourists asking to see her photo mobbed Kirsty. The local newspaper was called and the staff asked her to wait for them to come to interview her and take her photograph.

Kirsty said to her friends, 'Wow, after all this time my wish has come true. I can't wait to show the photo to Dad, Mum and Grant. I wonder how many newspapers will want to buy it?'

Chapter 14

Secrets

Meanwhile, back at the holiday castle Grant was welcoming guests for the surprise celebration. Being experts at putting on amazing parties, his parents were supervising the decorations and entertainment, and they were delighted to see their son so happy.

Robert turned on the television early in the afternoon to check what was going on in the world, and listened with wonder to the top local story, which had an amazing photo of a dragon-like creature. The newswoman was interviewing a familiar face, his daughter! He called out to everyone in the castle to hurry into the projection room.

There was great excitement amongst the guests as they saw Kirsty talking about Nessie and the photograph she had captured.

Although they all knew what a talented girl she was, this occasion promised her a great future as a photographer. It often only took one event to set up a person for life. Robert and Rebecca couldn't wait to see their daughter and view her picture of Nessie.

When the girls walked through the door some time later, Alinda was surprised and delighted to greet her friends at her party. She was touched that Grant had gone to such lengths to make her birthday special. Of course, after wishing Alinda a happy birthday, the guests naturally clamoured after Kirsty, who was enjoying the limelight. She was asked again and again to tell her story, but she never grew tired of it and, after putting the photos onto the big screen, took pleasure in the feeling of being the centre of attention.

This scoop would springboard her into the public eye with great career prospects as a celebrated photojournalist. She had almost forgotten her ambition, but it was just what she had craved after her first unsuccessful effort of photographing the elusive Loch Ness monster, so many years before.

Meanwhile, Alinda and Grant had taken advantage of the fact that the party was no longer about the birthday, and had slipped away. As this was their last evening in the castle before returning to London, Alinda wanted to visit her cavern for her final birthday treat.

Grant, wishing to finish off her day in perfect style, took her hand and led her to the jetty and the awaiting boat. Millie, ever watchful, followed them and as she sensed where they could be heading, jumped into her car and went ahead to Urquhart Castle. She sneaked down under the cover of darkness and waited near the jetty for the boat to arrive.

Grant wanted their journey up the loch to last forever. Under the soft moonlight, Alinda appeared to him to be even more beautiful. Her hair shone, her eyes sparkled and her manner towards him was receptive and warm. He took her hand, kissed it and said, 'I hope this has been a perfect birthday.'

For the first time since waking in this strange modern world, Alinda felt at peace, with Grant sitting beside her and her beloved Nessie swimming attentively alongside. Was this life to be her destiny?

Millie saw the boat approaching and knew her instincts had been correct. She was determined to find out why Urquhart Castle was such a magnet to Alinda and how she could use any additional information to her advantage.

As she watched, Grant helped Alinda alight and Millie noticed he continued holding her hand as they walked away from the boat. Jealousy filled her being. She was not surprised to see them walk towards the side of the castle and disappear.

Quickly she ran to the spot she had last seen them and found a fissure in the rock behind some vegetation. She eased herself into the space then tiptoed up the passage to avoid discovery. This time she would discover all Alinda's secrets.

Up ahead, oblivious to Millie's presence, Grant and Alinda greeted Nessie with exuberance. Alinda said she would not be back till the following year, and told Nessie she must remain in charge of her cavern till she returned.

At the back of her mind, Alinda had the passing thought that next time she was there she would have to make her decision. Would she stay or would she go?

Grant recognised the fleeting look of sadness on her face, reached out for her and pulled her close to him. He kissed her gently and was overwhelmed when she responded. In the shadows, Millie had seen everything. She was so shocked by her first view of the enormous monster, Nessie, that she almost missed the fact that Grant and Alinda had kissed.

Once she regained her composure, she was filled with the same overwhelming jealousy she had had in the past, but realised she had to remain hidden or be discovered, so she shrank back further into the darkness. Oblivious to the threat lurking in the cave, Alinda and Grant were nevertheless concerned when Nessie became agitated.

'Don't worry Nessie, I am not in danger, Grant is only showing me affection!' chuckled Alinda.

She did not understand why these words were of no comfort to the monster, but went to her chests and took the remaining gold and precious stones with her. Carefully she shut each chest, made certain her mirror was hidden and safe, and then bade Nessie and her cave farewell. Grant took her hand, and in a haze of happiness, they failed to notice that Millie was hiding in the shadows.

When Millie was certain they would not return and she felt it was safe to do so, she approached the chests with trepidation, keeping a watchful eye on the water where Nessie had so recently been. She tried to prise open the lid of the first chest she found, but a sudden bolt of energy threw her back. Picking herself up from the ground she realised there was a hidden power protecting the cavern and most probably Alinda.

She did not give up but explored further into the cave where she found what appeared to be a bed, and was excited to find a letter lying open upon it.

For once Alinda had not taken her usual care by making sure she left no trace of her past life. Millie sat down on the bed and began to read. Each sentence brought her closer to filling in the gaps of Alinda's secrets, which had her reeling at the enormity of what had happened.

She took out her camera and mapped the cave in digital images as her insurance to prove the reliability of this incredible story, although much to her annoyance, the monster had submerged so she had no evidence of her part in the story.

Leaving everything exactly as she had found it, apart from two souvenirs she put in her bag, she made her way back to reality.

On her journey back to the castle, Millie thought through her options. Her choice was clear.

During the next year, she would subtly encourage Alinda to make the choice to return to her home and past life. If instead she chose to stay with Grant, Millie would expose her story along with the photos she had taken of the letter and the trunks in the cavern.

This time she had the evidence of the photographs she had just taken along with the two items she had stolen, which had not been replaced in the trunks. She would not be made a fool of twice.

Chapter 15

Fame

Alinda was in love once again. Her feelings fuelled her creativity and her work was more in demand than ever. She was invited to show her creations all over the globe and with Millie as her personal publicist she selected venues for their character and charm, not for their status. Many important design houses begged her to show in their cities, but she chose obscure places that were small and intimate. They showed off her work with more adoration than financial gain, wanting to give their general public an ultimate experience of creative design. Inverness, which might be her last show forever, was booked as the final venue of the year.

From the sale of her parents' gold, Alinda had enough money to generate designs for the sheer joy of it rather than for material gain. However, her creations were inspirational and drew great crowds to view them. The increasing demand for her products created a dilemma for her. She felt in good conscience she could not take commissions that she would not be able to deliver beyond the following summer.

She remained torn between her new life and her old, but she never stopped missing her parents and sisters. Also, at quiet times she found herself looking back to her birthday when Andrew and she had become betrothed. If she went back would he still want her or would she be too late and find him already married to her friend Isla? She suffered from many sleepless nights. Although Grant was the most attentive and ardent sweetheart, and her work brought her great satisfaction and rewards, this modern day princess still felt there was a void in her life. Time was running out!

Millie, watching and waiting quietly for a sign that Alinda was swaying one way or another, cunningly planted seeds of doubt in her rival's mind, as to whether Grant was her one true love. She secretly worked all year on the 'perfect exposé' of Alinda's hidden life, always hoping she would never need to publish it. She believed if Alinda remained in her new time, that she would not be able to cope with the trauma of discovery and would isolate herself from her newfound existence and, hopefully, Grant!

Chapter 16

Urquhart Castle

During that whole year, Alinda was in a constant whirlwind of creation and travelling, and before she could draw breath her final show approached. She had seen sights and had experiences that were never even dreamed of in her life 500 years ago. An adoring public feted her and a delightful young man who was totally devoted to her squired her. What more could she want from life?

Grant drove her up through the glens to her last show in Inverness, following the same route of the year before. As they drove by Urquhart Castle a rush of nostalgia filled Alinda, increasing in intensity when she saw Nessie's outline under the water by the castle. It had been quite a year for them; fame favoured both. Nessie had managed to remain stealthily anonymous after Kirsty had published her photograph, evading the press by the same means as she had done for so many years in the past.

Alinda drew her future to the forefront of her mind; she could no longer ignore the decision she had to make. By her side in the car, Grant was also thinking of his prospects. What would his life be like without her if she left to return to her past? He would make her stay!

The Inverness exhibition was her most triumphant. It was also the most precious to Alinda, as her latest designs favoured her celtic past and were rapturously received. She had returned to her roots.

After the first show the couple went out to celebrate and discuss plans for her birthday the next day. She unsettled and hurt Grant when she told him of her decision to spend the night alone in her cavern, in the company of her dragon and her memories. He was filled with apprehension at this news and was frightened she would leave him without so much as a goodbye. However, thinking back through the happy year they had spent together, he dared to hope that this night would climax in her leaving her past behind.

Alinda asked him to meet her at the cavern at the break of dawn to give them time to discuss their future. Relieved, he agreed, as he had a sudden vision of an empty cave when he arrived, with no sign of either Alinda or of the love they had shared. There had been an unspoken agreement between them for the past twelve months to leave discussion of their futures alone. That rule had at last been broken.

Later, alone in the cave, she went to Nessie and whispered, 'Tomorrow you will be free from my service and you can choose to stay in this world or go back to the world of your childhood.'

On saying this she could think of nothing but the decision that she had to make, and she tried to remain awake all night trying to balance the old with the new. She re-read her mother's letter and took off her cameo necklace for the first time since her mother had placed it around her neck. The empty space where Andrew's picture had hung pierced her heart, and she searched frantically in the truck where she had thrown it the year before. Finding it, she stared at his familiar face. It resurrected her former feelings for him and she gently replaced it on the necklace, looked carefully at every detail of her family's faces, and then clasped it round her neck.

Next she found her mirror safe in its hiding place, and carefully took it out and placed it before her. Looking at the mirror for guidance, she felt no peace; all she saw staring back at her was her own reflection – a beautiful lost princess with the same piercing blue eyes and apricot hair she knew from long ago. Going over to one of her trunks she took out a nightdress, put it on and went to sleep with hope in her heart that her decision would be clear in the morning.

After Alinda had left him, Grant remained in the lobby of his hotel and was joined by Millie who knew from her careful observations that Alinda had gone.

They discussed the events of the day, then Millie asked him what was happening for Alinda's birthday. She betrayed no sign that she was fully aware of the magnitude of that day for them both.

'I am meeting her at Urquhart Castle early in the morning and we will spend the day together,' he answered.

Alarms rang in Millie's head. She feared she might have to publish the story of Sleeping Beauty's daughter after all. It would be an amazing tale for the world, which, although it would make her a household name, would destroy her relationship with Grant forever. It would have been so easy had he just loved her instead of Alinda! However, they parted easily as friends normally do, each knowing in their hearts that the following day would seal both their fates.

Chapter 17

Decisions

Grant tossed and turned all night. He was angry with himself for not asking Alinda outright to marry him. He knew that they loved each other but he wondered if he was enough to keep her from her family. Before dawn Grant set off for Urquhart Castle in his car. This time the journey was neither pleasant nor swift which was in stark contrast to the joyous trips he had taken with Alinda on many other occasions. His heart was filled with dread.

Alinda awakened to the sound of Nessie and her past calling out to her. Lying quietly, she relived the past two years of banishment brought about by the Shadow Fairy's evil christening wish. She mentally thanked the Virtue Fairies for their thoughtful gifts that had helped her through these challenging years. She was also grateful that her parents had put such an effort towards making her transition more bearable. The dilemma, which had been playing in the background of her thoughts for two years, now came to the fore with a mammoth force. She knew she loved Grant, who had guided her through the darkest of times, but she also recognised that Andrew had always remained important to her. She gazed over at the mirror and she began to doubt if indeed Faith Fairy would be able to keep her promise to fetch her home. Would the spell spun so long ago work, or was all Alinda's soul searching for nothing?

The moment of truth was fast approaching.

Alinda sat down stroking Nessie and waited for Grant. As he made his way to the car park for the last time, little did he know that Millie was following him. She watched him walk down the long path towards the Castle until he was no longer within her sight, then she sat down and began the long wait, either for his sole reappearance or the heartbreaking sight of Grant and Alinda together.

Nessie sensed that Grant was close at hand, alerting Alinda to his presence. She ran to him and gave him a warm embrace, then together they made their way towards the mirror. It was almost midday, as he had tarried on his momentous journey, and Grant knew he had little time left. He knelt down before her, asked her to marry him, and begged her not to go back.

Without warning, the mirror began to both shimmer and expand. Faith Fairy suddenly appeared within the frame of the mirror and stood with her hands outstretched. Alinda automatically ran towards her but stopped short of entering the mirror. Faith then said, 'Will you be coming home with me or will you be happier to stay here in your new life? Your family awaits you.'

Grant, feeling himself to be in the midst of a nightmare, got up and rushed towards the mirror, asking his love once again to marry him. Alinda, now with Nessie fast by her side, walked into the mirror, turned towards him and said, 'I'm going home, please come with me,' and she held out her hands for him to follow her.

'I've asked you twice to marry me, and you have not answered,' he replied.

He then hesitated and took a step backwards. The mirror shimmered and contracted and as they looked at each other one last time, Alinda was gone.

The
Sleeping Beauty

The Sleeping Beauty

A Traditional Tale

There was formerly, in the country known as Scotland, a king and a queen, having nothing to cloud their delight and love, but their want of children to share in their happiness. This was their whole concern: they contacted physicians, waters, vows and offerings to help them have a child, but for many seasons, none came to them. At last, however, after long waiting, a daughter was born. At the christening of the princess, seven fairies came to be her godmothers from the fairy kingdom. Each one gave her a gift.

The christening being over, a grand feast was prepared to entertain and thank the fairies; before each of them was placed a magnificent cover, with a spoon, a knife, and a fork, each made of pure gold set with precious stones and crafted with exquisite mastery. As they were all sitting down at the table, they saw come into the hall a very old but beautiful fairy. She had once been known by the name of Shadow. This Shadow fairy was not invited, because it was nearly one hundred years since she had been out of a certain tower, and was thought to have been dead.

The king ordered her a place to sit and because he had only seven settings made for the invited fairies, an unadorned cover was set before her at the table. The old fairy, thinking that she was slighted by not being treated in the same manner as the rest, murmured out some threats between her teeth.

One of the young fairies who sat by her overheard how she grumbled, and judging that she might give the little princess some unlucky gift, she went, as soon as she rose from the table, and hid herself behind the hangings, that she might speak last, and repair, as much as she possibly could, the evil which the fairy might intend.

In the meantime, all the fairies began to give their gifts to the princess in the following manner:

The youngest gave her gift that she should be the most beautiful maiden in the land.

The second, that she should have faith like an angel.

The third, that she should have grace in everything that she did.

The fourth, that she should sing like a nightingale.

The fifth, that she should dance like a flower in the wind.

And the sixth, that she would play on all kinds of musical instruments to the utmost degree of perfection.

The old fairy's turn coming next, she advanced forward, and with a shaking head, which seemed to show more spite than age, she said, 'The princess, when eighteen years old, will have her hand pierced with a spindle and die from the wound.' This terrible gift made the whole company tremble, and every one of them began to weep.

At this very instant the young fairy came out from behind the curtains and spoke these words aloud: 'Assure yourselves, O King and Queen, that your daughter shall not die of this disaster. It is true; I have not the power to undo what my elder fairy has done. The princess shall, indeed, pierce her hand with a spindle; but instead of dying, she shall only fall into a profound sleep, which shall last a hundred years, at the end of which time a king's son shall come and awake her from it.'

The king, to avoid this misfortune told by the old malicious fairy, caused at once his royal command to be issued forth, whereby every person was forbidden, upon pain of death, to spin with a distaff or spindle; nay, even so much as to have a spindle in any of their houses was forbidden.

About seventeen or eighteen years after, the king and queen being gone away to one of their castles in the lowlands of Scotland, the young princess happened one day to divert herself by wandering up and down the palace. When going up from one apartment to another, she at length came into a little room at the top of the tower overlooking Loch Ness, where an old woman, all alone, was spinning with her spindle. Now either she had not heard of the king's command issued forth against spindles, or else it was she, the wicked fairy who had taken up this disguise.

'What are you doing there?' asked Princess Aurora. 'I am spinning, my beautiful child,' replied the old woman. 'Ha,' said the princess, 'that is very amusing, how do you do it? May I see if I can do so, too?'

The old woman gave her the spindle and the yarn. She had no sooner taken it into her hands – whether being very hasty at it or somewhat awkward, or that the decree of the spiteful fairy had caused it, is not to be certainly known – than the spindle immediately ran into her hand, and she directly fell down upon the ground in a swoon. Thereupon the old woman cried out for help, and people came in from every quarter of the castle in great numbers; some threw water upon the princess's face, unlaced her, struck her on the palm of her hands, and rubbed her temples with water from the sacred well of the highlands. Nothing helped to awaken her.

The seventh good fairy that had saved her life by condemning her to sleep one hundred years was in the Land of Lessons Learned teaching virtues, when she was instantly informed of the accident that befell the princess. The fairy left her classroom immediately, and arrived at Urquhart Castle about an hour after the accident had occurred to Aurora. She was brought to the princess in an enchanted chariot drawn by three dragons.

The king and queen had also been sent an enchanted chariot. They had arrived moments before the good fairy. The king, seeing the fairy had landed, handed her out of the chariot. The king asked if the fairy could do a great favour for him and the queen. They wished that she would enchant the entire kingdom with a slumber spell. He thought that when the princess should awake, she might not know what to do with herself, being all alone in the old palace. Therefore, if she created with her wand such a spell, all the governesses, maids of honour, ladies of the bedchamber, gentlemen, officers, stewards, cooks, under-cooks, scullions, and guards, with their beefeaters, pages, and footmen would awaken with her. She agreed. She likewise decided to enchant all the horses that were in the stables, pads as well as others, and the great dog in the outer court, and the little terrier that lay by Aurora on the bed.

Immediately on her touching them they all fell asleep, that they might not wake before their mistress, and that they might be ready to wait upon her when she wanted them. The very spits at the fire, as full as they could be of partridges and pheasants, and everything in the castle, whether alive or not, fell asleep also.

All this was done in a moment, for the fairies are not long in doing their business.

And now the king and queen, having kissed their child without waking her, went very sorrowfully forth from the palace, and issued a command that no one should come near it. This however, was not needed; for, in less than a quarter of an hour, there got up all around the castle a vast number of trees, great and small bushes, and brambles, twined one within the other, that neither man nor beast could pass through, so that nothing could be seen but the very tops of the towers, and not that even, unless it were a good way off. Nobody doubted but that here was an extraordinary example of the fairies' art, that the princess, while she remained sleeping, might have nothing to fear from any curious people. The castle would return to its greatness when Aurora would awaken.

When a hundred years were gone and past, the son of a king then reigning, who was of another great royal clan, being out hunting in the highlands, asked about the towers that were on a hill overlooking the loch. Every one answered according as they had heard; some said it was an old ruinous castle haunted by spirits; others, that all the sorcerers and witches kept their Sabbath or weekly meetings within the great thick wood.

The most common opinion was that an ogre lived there, and that he carried thither all the little children he could catch, that he might feed them to his sea dragons. The prince was at a stand, not knowing what to believe, when an aged man spoke to him thus:

'May it please your highness, it is about fifty years since I heard from my father, who heard my grandfather say, that there was then in that castle a princess, the most beautiful that was ever seen; that she must sleep there for a hundred years, and would be awakened by a king's son, whom she was awaiting.'

The young prince was all on fire at these words, believing without considering the matter that he could put an end to this rare adventure; and pushed on by love and ambition, resolved that moment to attempt it.

Scarce had he advanced towards the hill, when all the great trees, the bushes, the brambles, gave way of their own accord, and let him pass through. He went up to the castle, which he saw at the end of a large avenue, and entered into it: what not a little surprised him was, he saw none of his entourage could follow him, because the trees closed again, as soon as he alone passed through them.

However, he did not cease from valiantly pursuing his way. He came into a spacious outward court, where everything he saw might have frozen up the hardiest person with horror. There reigned all over a most frightful silence, the image of death everywhere showing itself, and there was nothing to be seen but stretched out bodies of men and women, and animals, all seeming to be dead. He, however, very well knew by the rosy faces and the red noses of the beefeaters that they were only asleep; and their goblets, wherein still remained some few drops of wine, plainly showed that they had fallen asleep while drinking. He then, crossing a court paved with marble, went upstairs, and came into the guard chamber, where the guards were standing in their ranks, with their halberds on their shoulders, and snoring as loud as humanly possible. After that, he went through several rooms full of gentlemen and ladies asleep, some sitting and some standing.

At last he came into a chamber all gilt with gold; here he saw, upon a bed, the curtains of which were all open, the fairest sight that he had ever beheld, a beautiful maiden. She appeared to be a princess of about the age of eighteen, and whose resplendent beauty had in it something divine. He approached with trembling and admiration, and fell down before her on his knees. And now the enchantment was at an end. The princess awakened, and, looking at him kindly, said, 'Is it you, my prince? I have waited for you for such a long time.'

The prince, charmed with these words, and much more with the manner in which they were spoken, introduced himself as Prince Colin of Aberdeen. He said that he knew upon seeing her for the first time in her sweet slumber, that he loved her and hoped that she too, would love him. They then talked for four hours together and yet said not half of what they had hoped to say to each other.

In the meantime the entire palace awakened, every one thinking on his particular business. The chief lady of honour, being ready to die of hunger, grew very impatient, and told Aurora and Colin, aloud, that supper was served up. The prince then gave Aurora his hand; though her attire was very magnificent, his royal highness did not forget to tell her that she was dressed like his great-grandmother; but she looked not the less beautiful and charming for all that.

They went into the great chapel and were married by the priest. They then walked into the great hall of looking-glasses, where they held the wedding feast overlooking the great loch. The officers of the princess served them; the violins and hautboys played all old tunes, but very excellent, though it was now about a hundred years since they had any practice.

King Colin and Queen Aurora lived happily, until they faced the loss of their youngest daughter, Alinda.

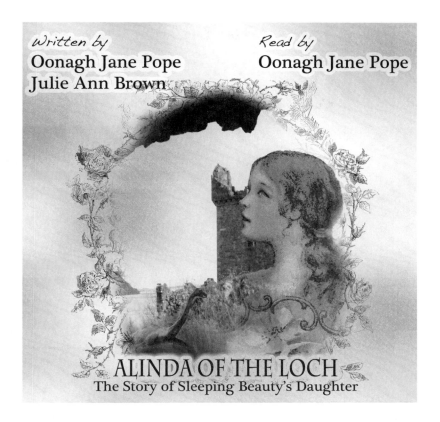

Written by
Oonagh Jane Pope
Julie Ann Brown

Read by
Oonagh Jane Pope

ALINDA OF THE LOCH
The Story of Sleeping Beauty's Daughter

Also available in audio form.

www.alindaoftheloch.com
www.alindaoftheloch.co.uk

Urquhart Castle
Gallery

Urquhart Castle lies on the shores of Loch Ness, which is the northernmost loch of those in the The Great Glen. This glen runs from Inverness in the north down to Fort William in the south. Loch Ness is over 200 metres deep with the hills around it rising to about the same height. Castle Urquhart was once one of Scotland's largest castles and it commands magnificent views up and down the loch. The position of the castle was perfect for early clans to keep a lookout in case of enemy action against them, and it saw many battles throughout it's history. You can find out more about that history by visiting our website.

www.alindaoftheloch.com